The Mighty Ducks:
The First Face-Off

Debra Mostow Zakarin

DISNEY
PRESS

New York

Printed in the United States of America.

First Edition

1 3 5 7 9 10 8 6 4 2

The text for this book is set in 16-point Berkeley Book.

Library of Congress Catalog Card Number: 96-71629

ISBN: 0-7868-4147-8

Chapter One

The crowd at Anaheim Pond is going wild.

"It looks like the Mighty Ducks' season-long winning streak may be coming to an end," says the announcer in the press booth overlooking the Anaheim skating rink. "They're tied with the Maine Quahogs with only seconds remaining. The Quahogs center, Jean-Luc, is guiding the puck

1

toward the Ducks' goal. He shoots and he misses! Wildwing's arm deflects the incoming puck.

"Wow! Wildwing racks up another record-breaking block and it's an incredible come-from-behind victory for the Mighty Ducks!" says the announcer, wiping the sweat from his brow. "Not only are these Ducks mighty, but they're also ducks!"

Wildwing, Nosedive, Mallory, Tanya, Grin, and Duke high-five one another. They skate off of the ice and into their box where they are greeted by their manager, Phil.

"That's my Ducks!! Way to go, boys," he says.

"Excuse me," says Mallory.

"Oops, sorry there, madam. Way to go, boys and ladies."

Phil proudly looks at his team—the Mighty Ducks. "Okay, you quack-pot hockey players. Dinner's on me tonight."

"You're all right by us," says Nosedive.

Wildwing, Nosedive, Tanya, Grin, Mallory, and Duke head out of the box.

"Going somewhere?" asks Captain Klegghorn, flashing his police ID to Phil. "I wanna have a word with you, Slick. Downtown!"

Klegghorn takes Phil's elbow and begins to escort him out of the Ducks' box.

"Rain check, babes!" Phil calls after the Ducks.

Down at the station, Phil tells Captain Klegghorn the Mighty Ducks story:

"They're from Puckworld," begins Phil, "which is very much like Earth, although the continents are shaped differently and are largely covered with snow. Everyone is a duck, and everybody plays hockey. Winter is all year long. Duck waiters skate around in

3

the restaurants and Duck patrons eat off of puck plates and use miniature hockey sticks as forks and knives."

"So, what you're saying is they eat hockey?" asks Klegghorn.

"That's right. And they sleep hockey and even think hockey. In school, the teacher uses a hockey stick as a pointer."

"And I'm assuming this teacher is a duck?" asks Klegghorn.

"You're getting it, Cap," says Phil.

"I'm getting nothing except for a lot of turkey talk. How did the Ducks leave this so-called Puckworld and get to Earth?"

"Will you let me tell the story at my own pace? Jeez," says an exasperated Phil.

Chapter Two

Phil continues to tell Klegghorn the story of the Mighty Ducks:

"Legend has it that the Saurian Overlords tried to conquer everything in the universe. And nobody was able to find them because the Saurians had evil magical powers. But then Drake DuCaine invented a special mask, a goalie mask. The Mask can see through the Saurians' invisible shields. Drake hunted down the evil Saurians with the Mask. He kicked their scaly tails into a whole other dimension. But one day an alien warship, the *Raptor*, came to Puckworld."

* * *

"We're in range of Puckworld, Lord Dragaunus," says Siege.

"Prepare to de-cloak . . . now!" yells Dragaunus.

Siege's burly hand presses a button. Suddenly, dark and menacing starships shimmer into view. They drop their invisible cloaks and start gliding downward toward the surface of Puckworld. All of the ships are identical except for the hawklike *Raptor*.

Dragaunus sits in the cockpit of the *Raptor*.

"I, Dragaunus, last of the Saurian Overlords, have escaped the dimensional limbo in which my ancestors were imprisoned, and now the descendants of Drake DuCaine shall pay for what he did to my ancestors!"

6

The starships zoom in on a building, fire some rays, and BOOM! An explosion. No more building.

"Technology freed us from that dimensional limbo, and technology will crush Puckworld flat!" says Dragaunus, laughing.

Soon, all the buildings in Puckworld are shattered, and the sky is gray and grim. Hunter drones patrol the streets.

Dragaunus puts all the Ducks to work in order to expand his takeover operation to include the whole galaxy. Dressed in nothing but rags, the Ducks trudge along the streets of Puckworld in single file.

Wildwing and his brother, Nosedive, trudge in one of these lines.

"'Dive," Wildwing whispers. "I can't take this much longer! Where is the Resistance we keep hearing about?"

"I hear ya, bro!" says Nosedive. "There's never a freedom fighter around when you need one!"

"If only I could get inside that Monitor Tower, I . . ." says Wildwing.

But suddenly, a hand grabs his shoulder and pulls him out of the line into an alley.

"Canard!" Wildwing says to his friend, who is dressed in a turquoise hockey jersey. "Where've you been all these months?"

"I'm with what's left of the military—in the Resistance!"

"The Resistance! It really exists?"

"You bet," says Canard. "I'm organizing a team of our best special forces and a few civilians we've had our eyes on, like you!"

Wildwing smiles.

"We're gonna take out Dragaunus!" says Canard.

"Nobody's ever seen him! How?" asks Wildwing.

"Because I found *it*."

"Found what? Where?" asks Wildwing.

"In an ancient tomb in the mountains they call Twin Beaks, I found the Mask!

8

Drake DuCaine's Mask!"

Canard reaches into his pack and pulls out the Mask.

"Didn't I tell you? Was Drake DuCaine the main Duck or what!" says Nosedive.

Canard and Wildwing jump with surprise.

"Beat it, Duck-boy," says Canard.

"No way! I wanna give that Saurian sleazoid some major payback," says Nosedive.

"Out of the question, Nosedive," says Canard. "You're too young, and this mission's much too important."

"If you want *me*, Canard, then my brother's part of the deal," Wildwing says, putting his arm around Nosedive.

"Okay, okay. But you're responsible for the kid's safety," Canard says, a bit annoyed.

"You got it," says Wildwing.

Chapter Three

Canard, Wildwing, and Nosedive peer around a street corner.

"Who else do you plan on recruiting?" asks Wildwing.

"Her," says Canard, pointing to a duck heavily armed and wearing commando gear.

"Leave them alone," yells Mallory.

The Drones twirl around. Their arms transform into blasters, and they charge toward her at high speed and open fire.

Mallory whips a bazooka up to her shoulder and plows into their midst.

"Take that, cyber-creeps!" Mallory yells.

"Did you see that," says an amazed Nosedive. "She reduced them to scrap metal in under four seconds!"

Canard smiles.

"Mallory McMallard?" he asks her.

"That depends. Who wants to know?"

"Puckworld's Special Forces," Canard says as he flashes an ID. "I want you to volunteer for a mission."

"Are you trying to ask me out on a date?" Mallory asks suspiciously.

"We're going after Dragaunus himself."

"Well, why didn't you say so in the first place," Mallory says, and salutes. "I'm ready for duty."

A huge Monitor Tower stomps along on its tripod legs as it patrols the streets. A Duck, dressed in black, grabs onto one of the tower's legs as it passes.

"Who's that?" asks Wildwing.

"That's an operative of ours named Tanya. She's a high-tech whiz," says Canard.

11

Tanya pulls out her Omnitool and aims it at a plate on the tower leg's hull. Then she pulls out a small remote-control device and presses a button.

The leg explodes and the Monitor topples to the street—an eruption of fire and debris.

"Nice work," says Canard.

"Thanks," says Tanya.

"Another chick? What is this, *Charlie's Ducklings*?" asks Nosedive.

"Hey there, little Duck-boy. If you don't stow that talk you're gonna get a beakful of knuckles!" says Mallory as she drapes her arm over Nosedive's shoulder and bats her eyes.

Suddenly, rays blast all around the Ducks.

"Enough of this small chick-chat. Maybe

we should get out of here before the Hunter Drones zap us and terminate our life functions," says Tanya.

The Ducks take cover and relax in an abandoned warehouse.

"Who's that?" asks Nosedive, pointing to the figure of a duck silhouetted in the window.

"Our next recruit," says Canard.

"Well, it looks as if our next recruit is jimmying the window open," says Wildwing.

"I should hope so. Our next recruit is none other than Duke L'Orange!" Canard says, smiling.

"But . . . but . . . he's the most notorious cat burglar on the planet!" says a shocked Wildwing.

"Yes. And that's exactly why we need him! Anyway, he's putting his skills to good use these days."

"Canard, old friend. Good to see you again!"

"We need you for a mission, Duke!"

"You can count on me," says Duke.

"We've got one last member to round up," says Canard.

In a small dingy room, which is sparsely decorated with oriental screens and scrolls, Grin sits in the lotus position.

"Grin! Have you taken leave of your senses?" asks Duke.

"The guy's a total space cadet," says Mallory.

"Maybe, but he can bend steel just by sneering at it," says Canard.

"I've been waiting for you," Grin says, standing. "Let's go."

The Ducks watch and listen to Canard very closely.

"We've got explosive pucks, grappling pucks, smoke screen pucks, and flash pucks," says Canard. "They can be thrown manually or deployed

14

from these puck guns."

"This is slammin' gear, Canard! We're set for some serious street hockey!" says Nosedive with great enthusiasm.

"Where did you find this ship?" asks Duke.

"It's the last of the military's Aerowings. The Resistance Forces managed to hide it when the Monitor Towers attacked," says Canard. He looks at his crew and shouts, "Let's pay Lord Dragaunus a visit!"

Chapter Four

Mallory, Wildwing, Nosedive, Grin, Duke, and Tanya are sitting in the *Aerowing* cockpit. Canard is at the controls. The *Aerowing* crosses over barren terrain outside of the city.

"The Monitors are controlled by a computer in Lord Dragaunus's headquarters," says Canard. "And that is our target."

"Have you ever seen Lord Dragaunus's headquarters?" asks Duke.

16

Carefully, Canard takes the Mask out of his pack and puts it on.

"I have," he says in a very deep voice.

"Why's his voice so deep?" asks Nosedive.

"Shh," says Wildwing. "It's because of the Mask."

"Now prepare yourselves! We're almost there!" Canard continues.

"Here?" yells Mallory. "We're twenty klicks from nowhere!"

"The Master Tower has an invisibility field around Lord Dragaunus's Cloak of Darkness!" Canard says.

Computerized data scrolls in the eyepiece of the Mask.

"And we're about to pass through it!"

Whoosh! The atmosphere seems to ripple. A huge high-tech black tower shimmers into view. Lord Dragaunus's headquarters.

The *Aerowing* lowers and lands next to the black tower. Canard, Wildwing, Duke,

Grin, Mallory, and Tanya emerge from the ramp. It closes behind them.

"Yo! What about me?" asks Nosedive, banging on the cockpit window.

"Somebody's gotta guard the ship, little bro! Be a team-playing Duck," says Wildwing, waving good-bye.

"I think I just got the short end of the hockey stick," Nosedive says to himself.

All the other Ducks are by the base of the tower. Duke looks up, draws his sword, and inspects the cable.

"I'll have us inside in a flash," Duke says. And no sooner said, than done, there's a *zap!*, followed by a *boom!*, and the whole portal explodes!

Duke ties the cable to the ragged end of an exposed girder and yells to the others, "Don't just stand

18

there preening your feathers. Come on."

Canard and the other Ducks start climbing the cable.

The Ducks, led by Canard, head deep into the tower. They are prepared to give Dragaunus a major shake-up. Canard is holding a small sensor device.

"According to our information," Canard says in his mask voice, "the main computer's heavily fortified."

"That's gotta be the understatement of the century," says Wildwing as he points to a pair of huge steel doors, which are closed in an interlocking geartooth configuration.

"Grin, you're on," says Canard.

Grin approaches the metal doors and grasps the seam with his fingertips.

19

"Mind over metal, mind over metal, mind over metal," Grin says over and over again.

Grrrr!! and he forces the doors wide open.

There is a vast chamber on the other side of the metal doors. On one side are sweeping banks of controls. On the other side are huge transparent columns. They are crackling with blue energy.

"The master computer!" shouts Canard. "Tanya, take Mallory and shut it down!"

Wildwing watches as Tanya and Mallory run through the doors and into the chamber.

"Canard," says Wildwing, "everyone has special skills. What am I doing here?"

"You're going to get Lord Dragaunus out so we can jump him," says Canard, still wearing the Mask.

"What?" gasps Wildwing.

"You're the decoy!"

"Why me? I've got a better idea. Let's use

a little painted wooden duck instead."

"You're the best goalie I know," says Canard. "You'll be able to take anything Lord Dragaunus can throw at you!"

Wildwing takes a deep breath and exhales. He starts off down the corridor.

"We'll be right behind you, buddy!" Canard yells.

Canard checks his watch and turns to Grin and Duke.

"We'll give him a thirty-second start and . . ." Canard stops mid-sentence and turns to the door sliding open behind him.

Siege and Chameleon appear.

"Well, so much for that plan, Canard," says Duke.

"All right—let's pluck some duck," shouts Siege.

A cloud of smoke boils

21

into existence and Wraith emerges from it.

"I've a better idea, Siege. Let's roast them," says Wraith as he cocks back his arm and hurls off a fireball.

Duke swats away the fireball with his saber and swipes at Wraith.

"Your powers don't frighten me, Saurian. *En garde!*"

Wraith evaporates. Duke blinks.

"Say! That *is* a neat trick," he says, astonished.

Siege raises a hand-held, lighted device, presses a button, and shimmers out of existence.

"Now you featherweights got no defense against us," shouts Siege.

"Oh, yeah? Don't tell me

you never heard of Drake DuCaine's Mask?" asks Canard.

Canard springs forward and grabs the invisible Siege. Siege shimmers back into existence as Canard grabs the device from his hand and throws it off. But Siege slams into Canard and sends him crashing into the wall.

Chapter Five

Wildwing is walking down the hallway of Dragaunus's command center talking to himself.

"You're the bait, ol' pal! 'You're the decoy!' Remind me to do *you* a favor sometime, Canard!"

Wildwing peers around a corner. Three Hunter Drones are standing in front of a huge steel doorway. They turn around and begin zapping rays at Wildwing. The rays zing off his armor. Wildwing thrusts his arm forward and starts firing pucks at the Hunter Drones.

Two Drones leap onto Wildwing and

grab his arms. Wildwing flings the Drone on his left arm against the wall and it shatters. He holds up the Drone on his right arm and from point-blank range fires a puck straight into it, literally blasting it to bits.

The last Drone leaps at Wildwing. Wildwing grabs it and hurls it against the command chamber doorway.

"That oughta get his attention!" says Wildwing as he wipes himself off.

The door slowly slides open. But there is nobody there. Wildwing shudders at the sound of evil laughter.

"Uh-oh. I got his attention," says Wildwing, running down the corridor.

"How disappointing! I was hoping it would be that pest Canard! He's been causing me trouble for months!" roars Dragaunus.

Something suddenly picks Wildwing up and he is sent crashing straight through a

25

wall and into a storage room. Wildwing picks himself up from a pile of crates and looks around worriedly.

"Okay, guys!" Wildwing says aloud. "Let's move in and nail this creep! Guys? Guys . . .? Ladies?"

Something with a claw picks Wildwing up by the front of his uniform. He dangles in midair.

"Your feathered friends aren't coming!" roars Dragaunus. "Nothing can save you now, Duck. You're mine!" He draws his lips back and reveals ragged rows of razor-sharp fangs.

Wildwing is brought to a wide chamber. He is bound by high-tech manacles and floats about fifteen feet in the air above a large empty steel ring on the floor.

26

Dragaunus stands in front of a control panel. He pulls a lever. A grid of blue-hot rays crackles within the big steel ring. Wildwing is slowly lowered toward the ring.

"When you hit those rays you'll be incinerated," says Dragaunus, smiling. "I've always had a fondness for crispy duck."

Wildwing looks down.

"I don't suppose I could interest you in a nice pasta salad instead?" asks Wildwing.

Meanwhile, Nosedive is in the cockpit of the *Aerowing*. He is feeling very frustrated at being left behind.

"If I could just get this heap in the air," says Nosedive aloud.

He eyes a red button on the controls and thinks for a moment about what he should do.

"Ah, a duck only lives once."

Nosedive pushes the red button and a pair of windshield wipers sweeps over the cockpit bubble in front of him.

"Oops! Wrong button."

Chapter Six

Tanya and Mallory are in the master computer room in the tower. Tanya is rapidly pressing buttons on the control panel. She hands Mallory an explosive pack.

"I've gotta warn you, Tanya," says Mallory. "Machines and me don't get along too well."

"That could be a good thing. Now, throw the toggle switch," instructs Tanya.

Mallory stares at the explosive-pack controls in her hand. There's a digital timer holding steady at 10:00. Below it is a red button and a blue toggle switch.

"I said," shouts Tanya, "throw the toggle switch."

"Uh, toggle switch . . . Affirmative."

Mallory presses the red button. *Beep, beep, beep* . . . The digital timer starts counting down at ten-times-normal speed.

"I told you to throw the switch, not press the button," shouts a frustrated Tanya.

"Switch, button—what's the dif?"

"The dif is about nine minutes of escape time."

Tanya and Mallory run outside as a fireball whips out the door and billows over their heads.

The explosion shakes the room where Wildwing is being held prisoner. He is only three feet away from the crackling beams below him.

Dragaunus hears the explosion and runs to check it out.

Back in the tower, Siege holds Grin by an arm and a leg and is swinging him around in a circle. He lets go and Grin goes flying.

"Stand still, you shape-shifting sick-o!" shouts Canard at Chameleon.

Chameleon ducks as Canard takes a swing at him. He shrinks down into a cute baby version of himself.

"I'm onwy twee an' a half years old!" Chameleon says innocently, but then he bulks into a huge bodybuilder version of himself.

"Kids grow up so fast these days!" Chameleon remarks as he slams Canard.

"Care to fight fire with fire?" Wraith asks Duke as he pulls out a blade of flame.

Duke and Wraith begin fencing. However, Duke's saber passes right through the fire blade!

Canard is on the floor when Siege moves toward him, cocking his tail back.

"Now, Duck," says Siege, "you are pressed lunch meat!"

But, suddenly, Grin grabs ahold of Siege's

tail. He jerks him around and flings Siege into Wraith and Chameleon. They fall down in a huge heap.

"Karma always gets you in the end," says Grin, smiling.

Siege, Wraith, and Chameleon pull themselves up and quickly run off.

Duke swings his sword and says, "Somehow that was just a little too easy!"

"Forget it. We've got to find Wildwing!" says Canard.

Chapter Seven

Wildwing is just inches above the ray grid! Canard, Duke, and Grin rush in.

"Oh, man! Just in time! My feathers are starting to sweat . . . ," Wildwing gasps.

Duke slings a grappling puck upward. The puck whips around one of the pipes on the ceiling. Duke swings, grabs Wildwing, draws his saber, and begins cutting Wildwing's bonds.

Boom! Tanya and Mallory run and join them.

"What's going on?" asks Canard in a *very* deep voice. "C'mon, troops! In thirty seconds we're all gonna be toast!"

The Ducks begin running out of the building. *Boom!* A wall explodes away.

"The *Aerowing's* gone!" exclaims Canard.

Angrily, Canard turns to Wildwing. "That kid brother of yours . . . ! No . . . this is all my fault!"

"Forget it!" Wildwing says. "We couldn't get to the *Aerowing* in time . . ."

Suddenly, the *Aerowing* roars up into view.

"Incorrectamundo, Ducks!" says a smiling Nosedive.

Nosedive extends the ramp and the Ducks run across it into the ship. The *Aerowing* roars upward as the entire tower is blown apart.

"Yeee-hah!!" shouts Nosedive.

"Look," shouts Duke, pointing.

The *Raptor* comes screaming out of its launch bay and heads up to the sky.

"The Monitors are finished! Puckworld's free again!" says Mallory.

"But Dragaunus is making a breakaway!" yells Wildwing.

"That's what he thinks," says Nosedive, steering the *Aerowing* in the direction of the *Raptor*.

Dragaunus is at the controls.

"Those feathered freaks are after us!" yells Siege.

"We shall escape them as we escaped that dimensional prison," Dragaunus says, pulling a large lever.

The electrode device on the *Raptor*'s prow fires a green ray, which creates a huge swirling vortex of light.

"What the heck is that?" asks Wildwing.

"His ship seems to be generating some

kind of dimensional gateway," explains Tanya.

"Say what? English, speak English," cries Nosedive.

"It's pretty technical, but Dragaunus is trying to escape into an alternate parallel dimension."

"Then we'll follow him," Wildwing shouts, pointing in the direction of the *Raptor*.

"C'mon, baby bro! Punch it!" shouts Wildwing. The Ducks are pushed back as Nosedive applies more thrust to the *Aerowing*.

The *Raptor* vanishes into the vortex. The *Aerowing* streaks through the swirling tunnel of psychedelic light.

"They're still on our tail," Siege says nervously.

"Then I'll destabilize the gateway!" Dragaunus says, operating the gateway's generator controls.

A small whirlwind of light suddenly swirls up out of nowhere and begins to grow larger next to the *Aerowing*. The Ducks look out of the *Aerowing's* cockpit.

"Tanya, what is that?" asks Wildwing.

"If I didn't know better I'd say that was an instability in the dimensional gateway," explains Tanya.

"Whoa! If that thing gets big enough it could swallow the ship!" says Duke.

"Isn't there some way to close it?" asks Wildwing.

Tanya shakes her head. "It won't shut down till it's consumed some form of matter!"

"We're going to have to jettison something . . ."

"Like what?" Tanya asks, interrupting Wildwing. "Everything's bolted down!"

Wildwing looks around.

"Canard! Where's Canard?" Wildwing shouts nervously.

Canard is standing behind the cockpit by the open hatch. Psychedelic lights are streaming by.

"Canard! What are you doing?" shouts Wildwing.

"You heard Tanya," Canard said with a deep voice. "I'm going to close that thing down! It's the only way!"

"Are you crazy?"

The whirlwind pulls Canard off his feet. Wildwing lunges and grabs the side of the hatch and extends his arm. Canard grabs it.

Canard pulls off the Mask with his free hand and holds it out to Wildwing.

"Take it, Wildwing," Canard says in his normal voice.

Wildwing, trembling, takes the Mask from Canard.

"You're team captain now!"

Canard lets go of Wildwing's arm.

"No-o-o . . . !!" Wildwing shouts in horror.

Canard goes spiraling down out of existence. Multicolored light continues to streak past the *Aerowing*.

Mallory, Grin, Duke, and Tanya gather around Wildwing.

"He sacrificed himself to save us!" says Duke.

"Truly an evolved soul," says Grin.

"Uh, guys," Nosedive yells to his fellow Ducks. "Those dino-creeps are getting away!"

The *Raptor* vanishes into a blazing point

of light at the distant end of the psychedelic tunnel.

"They must have passed through the other end of the gateway," says Tanya, pointing out of the cockpit window.

"Then that's where we're going. Punch it, Nosedive!" commands Wildwing.

Thunder cracks and lightning flashes across the sky over the suburbs of Anaheim, California.

"Where's the *Raptor*?" asks Mallory. "I can't get a visual."

"More to the point, Mallory—where are we?" asks Wildwing.

Chapter Eight

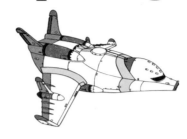

The *Aerowing* lands behind some empty hills near a suburban valley.

"Let's ditch the *Aerowing* here," says Wildwing, pointing out of the cockpit window. "We'll explore on foot."

Wildwing, Grin, Mallory, Nosedive, Tanya, and Duke begin walking down the street. All around them are town houses and condos. They come to a sign:

WELCOME TO ANAHEIM,

HOME OF THE MIGHTY FROGS.

Wildwing looks around and says, "It kind of looks like . . . like Puckworld!"

"Yeah, but with better weather," adds Mallory.

"Impossible," says Tanya. "We aren't even in our own universe anymore."

The Ducks keep on walking until they stand in front of a man who is sitting rather miserably in front of The Anaheim Pond. As their shadows fall upon him, he looks up and screams.

"Don't *do* that, fellas! The amusement park is across the freeway," he says.

"We're here to play hockey," says Wildwing.

"Why not. I don't have *nearly* enough aggravation in my life. The name's Phil."

Phil leads the Ducks to the locker room. He watches as they suit up in generic hockey gear. Wildwing puts on a real goalie's mask and places the Mask in a locker.

"See, my boss stiffed me," says Phil.

"Moved the whole team to Piscataway, New Jersey! If I can't get a new team soon, the city'll tear this place down—and I'll be out on the street!"

"Sorry to hear it, Phil," says Wildwing. "Now, can we play some hockey?"

"Oh, sure. Of course, you'll have to get past *them*, first. . . ."

Phil points to the rink where six tough-looking guys are skating on the rink.

"The Destroyers," Phil explains. "The worst goons in hockey. They've been kicked out of every league."

The Ducks skate in and the Destroyers are hysterical with laughter.

"A little early for Halloween, ain't it?" asks

the Destroyer captain.

"How 'bout a nice friendly game?" asks Wildwing.

"Sure!" says the Destroyer captain. "It'd be a pleasure to smear you all over the ice!"

Nosedive and one of the Destroyers face off as another Destroyer tosses the puck. The puck hits the ice and a third Destroyer skates in, slamming right into Nosedive as his opponent shoots the puck.

"Hey," yells Nosedive.

One Destroyer skates in and trips Tanya as another Destroyer charges in and high-sticks Duke. Three more Destroyers tackle Grin.

"See here, don't you have rules on this planet?" asks Duke.

"This isn't hockey," Mallory says. "It's a demolition derby!"

"I say we give these creeps some mega-payback!" suggests Nosedive.

"I'm with you, little brother, but we do it

by the book," says Wildwing, giving Nosedive a high five.

A Destroyer guides the puck along as Mallory gains on him. He swings his stick like a tomahawk, but Mallory ducks so low her chin nearly touches the ice as she steals the puck and passes it to Tanya.

Tanya skates forward with the puck as two Destroyers close in on her from either side. They raise their sticks to strike at her. With great agility, Tanya skirts around one of the incoming Destroyers as they swing their sticks and clobber each other!

Phil, alone in the stands, watches with complete interest.

"I have a gold mine on my hands," Phil says to himself. "Hockey-playing alien ducks!"

The Ducks *destroy* the Destroyers, so to speak, in hockey.

"Uh, Ducks," Phil says. "We gotta talk."

Chapter Nine

> **WELCOME TO ANAHEIM,**
> **HOME OF THE MIGHTY DUCKS.**

A workman takes down the sign WELCOME TO ANAHEIM, HOME OF THE MIGHTY FROGS and replaces it with WELCOME TO ANAHEIM, HOME OF THE MIGHTY DUCKS.

Phil and the Ducks are hanging out in the equipment room. Wildwing pulls out various puck-firing paraphernalia and frosted clear riot shields, puck bazookas, puck cannons, and ice shields.

"Now we're ready for anything Dragaunus can throw at us," Wildwing says. "Assuming we ever find him!"

"Wildwing," Duke says, "Canard made you leader before he disappeared into that dimensional vortex."

"No! I'm only . . . ," Wildwing says without confidence. "I'm only interim, temporary, acting leader until we can get him back."

"The bird who stays in his nest will never touch the sky," says Grin.

Wildwing stares at Grin for a moment.

"Hey, am I going nuts or is he starting to make sense?" Wildwing asks, pointing at Grin.

"He is making sense and, frankly, I always thought you were a little wacko," says Nosedive.

"Well, this bird's not going to sit on the nest any longer! Let's get moving!" Wildwing says.

"We'll take our new vehicle—the *Migrator*," says Nosedive.

The Ducks run out.

"Hey," Phil calls after them, "show a little mercy. This is costing a fortune! What about my perks? My expense account?"

"What about the evil overlord who wants to conquer the universe?" asks Mallory.

"Let him make his own merchandising deals," Phil says, pouting. "You can't run off in the middle of the night! You've got that dog-food endorsement tomorrow!"

Phil sighs and grabs his hair in frustration.

"I hadda hire a team of Ducks! Next time—wombats! They're easier to train."

The Ducks take their seats in the *Migrator* cockpit.

Outside the Anaheim Pond parking lot, a billboard folds back. It becomes two door panels in the ground, which slide open. The *Migrator* comes roaring out from an underground ramp.

"We're gonna find that Saurian sleazebucket and take him down!" yells Wildwing.

Chapter Ten

But the Ducks don't find Dragaunus, and after a very long evening they head back to their headquarters. Tanya is working at an open panel on a massive console. Phil is keeping her company.

"So, how was your evening?" asks Phil.

"Oh, you know," says Nosedive. "The usual."

"We threw out some garbage, deposited some bank robbers in a vault, and destroyed an invincible mindbender. Nothing special," says Duke, shrugging.

"Just great," mutters Phil to himself. "Hockey players by day—crime fighters by night!"

"Did you say something, Phil?" asks Mallory.

"Yeah. There's gotta be some way I can make this pay," he says, scratching his head. "I know! 'Official Mighty Ducks Secret Headquarters Tour!' Ten bucks a head."

"You lead a rich fantasy life there, ol' Phil," says Duke.

Nosedive looks over at Tanya.

"Nice mainframe," he says, smiling.

Tanya closes the panel of the console she is working at.

"I'm calling it 'Drake One!' We can use it to search for Dragaunus anytime you like. Like, even now," says Tanya.

"Wildwing," says Duke. "It's time you put the Mask on and started acting like a leader!"

"I'm just keeping it until we find Canard."

Duke shakes his head.

"He gave you the Mask for a reason! He wanted you to lead us!"

Wildwing drops his head.

"I'm not cut out to be a leader, Duke. It's too much responsibility."

BEEP-BEEP-BEEP-BEEP-BEEP!

"Drake One is picking up an unusually big energy source outside of the city," says Tanya. "Wildwing, it could be the *Raptor's* drive system."

"If you're right, then we've found Dragaunus!" exclaims Wildwing.

"Come on now," says Phil. "There are more important things than fighting evil. Like personal appearances and television . . ."

"You don't think this is important, Phil?" asks Wildwing. "Then see for yourself."

Wildwing grabs Phil's arm, drags him inside of the *Aerowing* cockpit, and straps him down in the seat next to him.

"It's okay. I believe ya," shouts a frightened Phil.

"Commence launch sequence!" commands Wildwing.

"Launch sequence engaged," answers Tanya.

The underside of the ice rotates into position and turns into a launch ramp.

"Full power to thrusters!" shouts Wildwing.

"Bustin' thrusters!" answers Nosedive.

Flames shoot out of the back of the ship! The roof of the Anaheim Pond splits and retracts. The *Aerowing* comes roaring out and heads up into the sky. It lands on a mountain.

"We're never going to find Dragaunus," says a disappointed Wildwing.

"Oh, yeah? Looks like he just found us!" screams Mallory. The *Raptor* heads right toward the Ducks and begins firing massive rays at the *Aerowing*.

Phil is panicked. He starts banging on the door of the *Aerowing*.

"I wanna go home! I wanna go home!" he cries.

"Are you wacko? That guy's packin' enough heat to charbroil the planet!" says Nosedive.

"And its gateway generator is our ticket home! We've got to get control of that ship!" says Wildwing.

The *Aerowing* attaches to the top of the *Raptor*.

"Wait here, Phil," says Wildwing. "We'll check it out."

"No prob, babe," says a shaking Phil.

The Ducks enter a large cargo bay filled with high-tech storage containers, crates, and metal drums. Dragaunus fires a ray from a device on his wrist. Duke, Nosedive, and Mallory are knocked backward into a stack of containers. It collapses around them.

Dragaunus turns toward Wildwing. He holds up a lighted device and presses a button on it.

"You won't even know what hit you," Dragaunus says.

Something invisible slams into Wildwing. He goes flying but quickly picks himself up.

"You can't hide, Dragaunus! You're going to lose!"

"How?" asks Dragaunus. "Your leader is gone and you're a poor substitute!"

"I'll find Canard. Whatever it takes," promises Wildwing.

"You pathetic fool! You'll never see your friend again!" says Dragaunus as he

slams Wildwing against the wall.

"No!" yells Wildwing. "I don't believe you!"

"Deal with it, Duck-boy! Canard is trapped for all eternity in dimensional limbo—along with the Mask!" says Dragaunus, laughing.

Wildwing whips out the Mask from his pack and puts it on.

"Wrong, dino-breath," Wildwing says in a very deep voice.

Dragaunus shimmers into view. He lunges at Wildwing. They are locked in a desperate struggle.

The other Ducks immediately run to the *Aerowing* as Dragaunus lets Wildwing go so that he can assume the *Raptor*'s control panel, and make his escape.

Chasing after the *Raptor* in the *Aerowing*, Tanya says nervously, "Uh, guys—I'm afraid we kinda destroyed the main engine. It . . . er . . . seems that we're sorta . . . gonna . . . crash!"

"But we've got to search for Dragaunus!" yells Wildwing.

"We can't, Wildwing," explains Tanya. "We don't have much fuel left."

Duke puts his arm around Wildwing. "We'll find them again, old friend, because now we have a leader!" he says.

Dragaunus rushes into the *Raptor* command chamber. "We can't go on like this forever, limping from one hiding place to another on impulse power!" he says.

"And sooner or later the Ducks will spot us with the Mask," says Siege.

"As long as the Mighty Ducks stand in our way, I fear the worst!" says Wraith.

"They won't stand in our way for long," says Dragaunus, curling up his lip in an evil sneer. "One day I'll pick my teeth with the wishbones of those meddling mallards."

"But that's another story, for another time," says Phil to Captain Klegghorn, "and I gotta go. I've got endorsement deals to sign up."

GET A FREE ISSUE OF

The fun-filled magazine that kids enjoy and parents applaud.

A whopping one million kids ages 7 to 14 are dedicated to reading Disney Adventures—you will be, too!

Each month DA plugs kids into super-charged fun...

- The inside scoop on movie stars and athletes
- Hot, new video games and how to beat 'em
- The characters they love
- Stories about everyday kids
- *PLUS:* puzzles, contests, trivia, comics, and much, much more!

- -

Notes:

My Doodle Page:

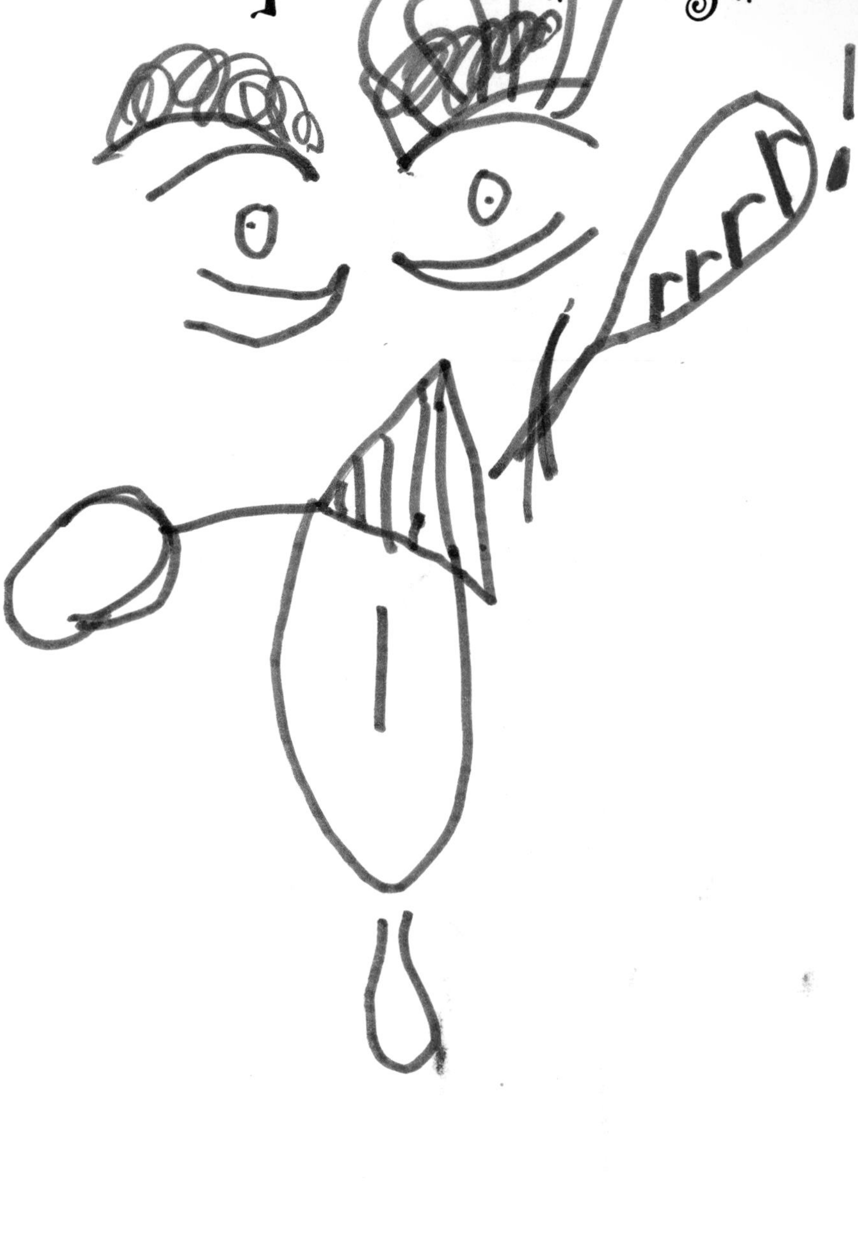